OBSCURE NARRATIVE

A POETRY COLLECTION

Heider Broisler

2021

Table of Contents

Autumn

A note reminded me of a scene;

a scene remitted me to fragments

that move around a core called life.

Tenderness and melancholy escorted us on autumn mornings ——

we could hear the winter.

Satie ... no one had understood autumn like him;

nobody had loved the autumn like her ——

life had faded:

autumn was preparing to say goodbye to her.

Worthy! I thought ... my hand was holding the coffin handle,

tears washed my eyes.

Gymnopédies ... Gymnopédies ... she whispered, convinced ——

days before she was consumed by the disease.

The coffin went down in the leaves' rhythm

that committed suicide from the trees.

Autumn was saying goodbye...

the priest prayed, but few pledged to listen;

Satie has overcome his words;

the coffin reached its destination....

Autumn will never be the same.

The Mirror Doesn't Lie

I smell the past when I enter that room:

an obscure passage in time

that no one else can see.

The old mirror abandoned in the dirty corner

confronts my character, so punished by time —

something sad to see.

I! Who is this person that persecutes me so much?

It is useless to unload all anger about life

when my own image torments me.

Dissimulation — that's all I see.

A life full of perfect performances — nothing is real.

The haughtiness had pasted on my skin;

happiness slipped through my fingers;

I camouflage myself under false maturity

that feeds on my body.

Dishonor accompanies physical death until the last breath.

My story is based on invisible pillars to the naked eye;

so deep that no one notices the deformities that

hide in my bowels.

It is easy to hide from others, less from yourself.

Damn mirror! Leave me alone with my illusions —

emotional wounds don't heal.

I cannot accept the truth;

I will break this old mirror,

so I will never need to stare at myself.

Fragments of Life

The seasons say goodbye without saying goodbye.

I am at peace when I make peace with loneliness,

I can only hear my thoughts during dinner.

It is so despicable to let my old aspirations

be silenced while a new spring welcomes me.

The sun gives life to the old garden stuck on the land;

fixed for a long time in the same place,

so changeable before the seasons.

I am not able to adapt like the flowers;

it's so beautiful to see them dance to the rhythm of the wind —

no disappointments and suffering.

I age with my loved ones;

my actions do not survive time.

I envy the flowers:

little lives honored for the next four months.

Poor me! I go shopping; I go to parties and dinners,

but I will never have a season just for me.

Four months ... it's not much...

it is enough to spare them from human frustrations.

My time is a dream collection that disintegrates

like old clothes.

The Old Doll

Investigating the old wooden chest full of old things that no

longer serve me anymore, I found my first best friend: Leah —

old friend always at my disposal

to hear my girl's confessions.

The doll smell reminded me memories of a distressing

childhood flooded with diffused dreams;

a commoner girl's daydreams

in which life would teach her the difficult

mission of being a princess.

The adults were useless. My friends dazzled by other

interests while I clung to edge of the abyss.

My ambitions hid in my ideas' little castle in which

I was the time's princess.

No! Enough of princesses:

'I free up the time so that my ideas can accommodate

themselves in its greatness.'

Leah doesn't judge my weaknesses;

she stares at me,

but in a human and comfortable way.

Dolls confide dreams that one day will become utopias;

my castle walls collapsed when I changed Leah

for friends who corrupted my life

forbidding me to dream like a girl.

Life had become a pragmatic ocean.

Everyone listens to me, but nobody understands me —

I just feel trained to live.

Where do the girl's dreams go?

Emily

She welcomed the time like no one else.
Faced with so many options, time just felt at
peace when it could share with her a
flow of events full of internal reflections,
carefree with trivial issues...
no one was as intimate to time as she was.
Unfortunately, her thoughts and feelings,
which dodged under that pale skin,
accompanied her for eternity, leaving us
all orphans of a mysterious beauty without equal.
I'd wish I had witnessed that sweet and silent woman
to walk by those hills as she listened to the cold wind
to caress her face, whispering to her fragments
of perceptions that only she could unveil.
There is no end! No, the existence of an end is not
compatible with that sublime genius that one day
it walked through this land full of miserable people...
Emily had a sensitivity that knew to coexist in peace
with her reason and feelings, giving her the power to
adjust time and space so she could unravel the minutiae
that life hides from ordinary people, or not worthy...
how many mysteries and pleasures could I find behind
those professorial eyes?
She did not surrender to dogmas or rules that prevent us
to dream and reflect on the subtleties that lurk among
the loopholes of freedom, with which she dialogued
while walking on those hills — she loved her family;
however, she felt truly free when
she immersed herself in the depths of her own mind —

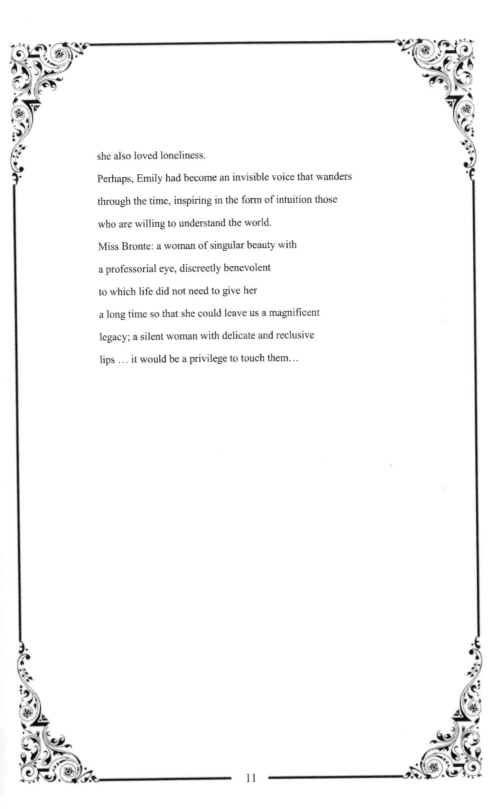

she also loved loneliness.

Perhaps, Emily had become an invisible voice that wanders

through the time, inspiring in the form of intuition those

who are willing to understand the world.

Miss Bronte: a woman of singular beauty with

a professorial eye, discreetly benevolent

to which life did not need to give her

a long time so that she could leave us a magnificent

legacy; a silent woman with delicate and reclusive

lips ... it would be a privilege to touch them...

The Shape of Jazz to Come

Mr. Coleman exceeded the limits overflowing a river of
envy, very common among mortals, in the minds of those
who saw him on the stage when his music ran through the
nights of the metropolis —— so thirsty for pleasure.

Mr. Coleman confused the minds of his great contemporaries
leaving them on a battlefield against a
conservative resistance, which neither they
didn't know they owned.

It may be a defective gene asleep
that woke up to contest
Coleman's rare genius.
Geniuses are not immune to stingy feelings.

In a dirty, dark and depressing room hid the
glorious past of a young, white homecoming queen who
had been convinced that she would have a splendid future
ahead of her — an America just for her…

the flowers died. The dream became a nightmare:
'Lonely Woman' opened the journey leading us to an
unique pain that sent us to a filthy, cheap hotel room
in which hopelessness stays every night.

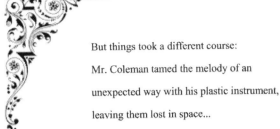

But things took a different course:
Mr. Coleman tamed the melody of an
unexpected way with his plastic instrument,
leaving them lost in space...

'Eventually' removed our minds from that cheap hotel
for the madness of a city that didn't pretend to be perfect
in the eyes of the Devil. The night does not belong to God —
he or she could not punish us.

The melody was more valuable than any suburban
dream full of hidden addictions written in false
virtues. But things have calmed down;
the music had changed again...

'Peace' carried us into an illusory calm;
a stop just to breathe, to relax,
while music opened the door to experiences
pre-psychedelic — Mr. Coleman called for change.

Other geniuses wallowed in envy while that
incredible quartet led by Coleman scandalized
a city full of open wounds.
The music never ceased to surprise…

'Focus on Sanity' showed us the strength of the marriage
between beat and rhythm, disharmoniously planned, that
divided opinions leaving no one indifferent,
for both good and for bad.

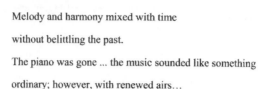

Melody and harmony mixed with time

without belittling the past.

The piano was gone ... the music sounded like something

ordinary; however, with renewed airs…

'Congeniality' has taken us to the recent past,

but renewed making many black geniuses suffer,

but there was light. Overcoming was on the way.

Nothing had been ignored, but times were different.

1959: the music would never be the same.

Some people abandoned — enraged by their own pride —

the place unable to admit who they witnessed

the birth of a genius…

'Chronology' got drunk them with both feet

at the edge of the abyss, leaving them perplexed and addicted

in those chords, forcing them to accept that not only

jazz musicians would drink from that source.

Applause to Coleman, Cherry, Haden and Higgins.

An Invisible Woman

Her dream has been silenced;

a girl lent to a generous rich family.

Poor girl ... sentenced to mop the floor

marked by fortunate children's footprints.

She scrubbed and scrubbed that noble wooden floor

while listening to the master's children share palpable

dreams as a rock.

The girl metamorphosed into a woman while

her dreams were falling apart like a fragile house,

that had been invaded by time.

The noble family guaranteed her the illusory safety comfort

in exchange for a loyalty that disintegrated her own identity.

Poor woman ... sentenced to display an uninterrupted smile

while she witnessed fate filling them with blessings.

There is no way to relieve a woman's pain, which has lost her

own brilliance in favor of a discretion that could cheat to death;

a lifeless existence built on invisibility.

The woman aged, but she was not forgotten:

the master's grandchildren guaranteed her right to

bury what has remained of her dignity in a cozy rest home —

a perfect place for those who have no history, legacy or

heritage ... at least, she will no longer be invisible.

Smiling

Smiles ... oh! Countless false purposes
that hide behind such a beautiful act.
Life reveals itself to a child who,
at the purity's apogee, is saddened
before men and women.

Blurred dreams, hands apart, head down low
life goes by a cold path that freezes hopes.
Smiles ... oh! What will it be this time?
'I don't like this. The last one who smiled at me
disdained my fragile ambitions.'

Minds and hearts handcuffed by a chaotic caste
that has never seen the light's singleness;
the flowers dancing in the wind.
'Don't simulate joy drenched in nefarious thoughts.'
Smiles ... oh! Be careful with who finds joy
in caressing the ego of others.

All that remains is to flirt with an existence illusion
that remits us to the denial
of feasible dreams, satisfying us with perfect slavery.
Wasting time —— no time to relax to the drops' sounds
that slide down the window…. Smiles...
oh! 'I wish they were true.'

My Lai Massacre

March 16, 1968

Deaths, rapes and mutilations of miserable individuals,
victims of a nation addicted to the desire for power;
proud to expose a white culture so tacky that
makes our brains hurt…

a village massacred by a nation that thinks it owns
of the monopoly of an illusory democracy in which it closed
its eyes while imposing segregation on blacks:
fathers and mothers of an incomparable global culture.

U.S. Army soldiers: butcher men to make Charles Manson
envy them — Charles … son of a nation that loves to glorify
serial killers … Charlie Company: cowardly boy-men who grew
up between a bible and a gun…

what to expect from a nation that manufactures indoctrinated
individuals to defend a monstrous illusory democracy
that despises and fears a diversity of ethnicities and customs?
Who did elect these sons of bitches, the Sheriffs of the world?

Men who could legally kill to defend
a lifestyle that only serves to feed
the wealth dream of the poorest.
They got rid of the courts, but not the history.

Men like these took revenge on the world to
hide — from everyone and from themselves — a
vulnerable mediocrity that made them incapable of a worthy
legacy. They hid behind their uniforms.

Men like these just give birth feelings of
destruction because they were unable to understand
the transformations that shape the world over time;
war lovers: men devoid of talent and wisdom.

The Captain saw about those poor non-Christian Orientals
his chance to avenge himself on the humiliations he had
received from white people: he hated himself.
Finally, he stank just like his old oppressors.

The Lieutenant saw about those poor non-Christian Orientals
his chance to avenge himself on the feeling of inferiority
that accompanied him throughout his life. A man of
low intellectual quotient who gave off incompetence.

Men like these are the fruit of hateful discipline
followed by military arrogance, fueled by a feeling
patriarchal that causes shame to many men.
Charlie Company's men had failed miserably as human beings.

The Funeral

It was a disappointment to see them beside my coffin.

The widow rested her thoughts beside a man who

had just come out from a melodramatic soap opera;

he could barely contain the satisfaction of seeing my remains

professionally accommodated in that terrible box —

he was a terrible actor,

maybe he played better when he was in bed.

'I will not blame myself for that. No matter my dead condition;

I'll never agree that all husbands are guilty of female betrayals.

No! No! I died, but I'm still a worthy man.'

My son couldn't face the coffin:

it was sad to see those lifeless eyes tamed by drugs —

my only son will be an unhappy man who will end

his days in a cheap hotel room.

The priest's useless sermon ceased: a man who had just

escaped from the law's clutches by practicing pedophilic acts.

My coffin went down slowly while my sister prayed

in the hope of a generous testament;

No! There was not one. I hadn't planned my death,

but a fair divorce.

My coffin reached its destination.

Time passes slower after death,

but that does not guarantee peace for me.

Dear Cowell

The world does not mourn your end,

your actions were as expressionless as your dreams.

Dreams? Or a cowardly man's nightmares limited

to his own insignificance?

You struggled, but you failed before you started;

your victims did not fail.

You have not gone beyond the empty-living individuals'

collective media hysteria in search of attention.

Theodore ... Theodore ... your friendly smile only served

to hide your inevitable fear: your failure.

You struggled, but you lived in the strongest ones' shadows;

your victims did shine.

The image of those young women conceived for the

success freeing themselves from their predecessors'

semi-slavery hurt your fragile ego devoid of talent;

a man unable to build his own destiny...

you struggled, but you were a fool before women;

your victims ignored you.

Theodore ... Theodore ... it was desperate for you to look at

yourself without finding anything of value.

Failure has accompanied you from your first steps;

you were born to weaken in your own insecurities.

You struggled, but you fell before the first obstacles;

your victims won.

Abyss

The enjoyment of seeing you in despair before the life

obstacles led me to taste what would be my own failure.

Yes, failure. Why not? Is there a greater human failure than to

delight in the despair of others?

Incomplete! This was the word that would define a whole life

full of obstacles skillfully constructed to sabotage myself,

without ever diverting (my) thoughts from your beautiful and

happy image, which always walked with long steps hand

in hand with life.

My conscience made me fool when I rationalized mountains of

false feelings for you, leading me to believe that you drowned in

a well of sadness created (desired) by my mind.

You got rid of the failure that so enjoy walking

through the halls and rooms of minds at war with their

own consciences — the first step in meeting failure is to ignore

the advice of the unconscious.

The enjoyment of seeing you in despair only passed through

abstract streets, why not virtual, on which only the weak and

dissimulated people pass through...

you built your own path — a simple, desperate desire

never got a chance to bring you down.

Bitterness

It's an invisible disease without face and pain that
accompanies us as a gap unresolved by the designers
of this universe so cruel and mysterious.

It's an echo echoing in collusion with time propagating
hidden interests even before the origin of all sins.
Why had everything been planned so obscurely?

The emotion persuades the reason, preventing us
to erase the past that acts like a tireless soldier to demoralize us
before a set of actions and useless thoughts.

Why are small scenes in life, which will never have value,
faced with the immensity of eternity (small scenes; yes, small
like their damn characters), matter so much?

The echo of characters — almost imperceptible to those who
designed the shape (cause and effect of our thoughts) —,
unfortunately, they move freely in our consciousness.

We are not able to eliminate or demystify rot
that is hidden in this gap present in all of us to which
prevents us acting with elegance and wisdom.

No-Self

My conceptions transmuted themselves through those

eyes brown — so immaculate...

the first changes were subtle,

thoughts disorganized themselves intuiting what was

to come: a repressed psychosexual battle.

My psyche came across strange insights;

slow and progressive mutations transformed me

while my personality struggled to survive;

I felt my valuable dogmas bleed

before my eyes.

'I feel strange ... my actions and decisions go through by

the sieve of her convictions. Did I change that much?'

My existence didn't disappear, but it had transformed itself with

every wisdom fragment resident

in the mind-face of that woman.

My judgments surrendered to the words that

ran down from that penetrating stare.

However, it was not enough to live under her ethics —

the process would be completed with the bed's warmth,

there had never been a battle, but the possession of my being.

The Small House on the Hill

The dining room had been properly prepared for

distinguished guests: a cardinal who did not take

his hungry eyes off the youngest son of the hosts;

a mayor who received illegal funds from construction

entrepreneurs linked to shady deals with her husband; a judge

who received money to prevent large polluting companies being

ordered to pay extremely high environmental indemnities;

a best-selling writer and activist who browsed the dark web to

pay for child pornography, and last but not least disgusting, a

senator who was a shareholder in a company that hired

semi-slave labor in Southeast Asia.

Behold here, ladies and gentlemen, another glorious night

under the roof of a majestic house full of wealthy people

who feed on greed and dark dreams.

Hosts and illustrious guests laughed at futile things —

while the signs of aging on those faces impoverished by

incoherence and falsehood of every parasitic being, which

sucks up hopes of humanity — focused on the intention to

mask a nefarious past that would not leave the future smile.

No! Not in that dining room....

'Why do majestic houses to shelter empty bodies of human

elements in which open our minds to small gestures that light

our steps?'

Illustrious people who survive at the expense of a

beautiful catchphrase ... the world deserves more than that!

The living room had been properly prepared for the

distinguished guests to relax after the glorious dinner

at which had become a ring without winners.

Those who only crave power are unable

to beat their own egos!

At a certain point, the cardinal watched the beautiful starry sky,

admiring it as if it were the great work of the creator, to whom

the cardinal begged for forgiveness every night due to his

almost insatiable desire for young men.

The cardinal forgot God for a few seconds when he noticed a

small house at the top of the hill.

'Is that little house on your property, Mr. Marshall?' asked the

cardinal. The host gestured an evasive 'no'. The mayor

approached the window. And she commented that the little

house seemed like a lovely place.

However, those horrible signs of aging — that not all the

wealth in the world can hide — soon emerged as if they were all

in front of a putrefying body when Mrs. Marshall informed them

that her husband and she had made an irrefutable offer for the

property; however, the owners of the place — miserable and

barbarians' foreigners — refused to sell it.

'That house would be ideal for my painting studio. I like privacy

to better be inspired by my art,' the hostess said, with her face

shaped by a slight feeling of disappointment.

They all approached the windows to get a better look at the

small house at the top of the hill.

They saw it; however, they were unable to feel and understand

the magic that rose from those walls:

the harmony originated from good thoughts that

routinely filled those people, perhaps rustic when they dealt

with their words, but full of wise actions.

Those noble and powerful individuals could not see — from

those distant windows in the living room — the real reason

by which the natural logic of life grants us real happiness

that can never be bought or corrupted.

That small house on the hill gave their owners a home cozier

than any wealthy family could dream of.

Those walls were also built of little secrets; however, they were

almost pure — almost naive — for the most part, good and

true ... an unreachable reality for those who live with the

pain of an eternal wound fed by the thirst for power.

The Town Lives

The rain had tamed; the water still runs down the streets

dragging dirt and small disposable things.

The air is more pleasant for those who have no roof.

The water washes the town's face like tears lamenting

the scorn that conducts to the mismatch of benevolent actions.

Streets are like scars that guide us to the consciousness illusion;

restlessness prevents us from intuiting

what the constructions have to tell us.

We guide ourselves by the desire of everything now;

the town had been coerced into destroying people and designs

confining them to prisons that fill them with self-confidence,

but so fragile before the inevitable.

The town does not understand why it was born under

'apartheid', minutely architected by urban

planners motivated by their superiority illusion.

The town seems more harmonious in the eyes of

those who fly over it.

Large and small buildings seem to embrace

each other as old friends.

Small beings with great aspirations move through

streets and sidewalks, without looking at each other, towards the

neighborhoods full of anxious and territorial concepts;

from above, everything seems to make sense:

parks and trees circumvent the despair that fuels

the daily violence;

cars, drugs and prostitution compete with shop windows

decorated for festive dates.

The town modernizes itself, mobilizes itself,

but does not humanize itself —

the rain's tears run only down the buildings.

Nothing but Reflexes

Knocking door to door looking for a tiny friendly gesture

the Being does not find individuals nourished

by benevolence, but mere drafts.

The Being is invisible to the eyes of those who were

hoodwinked by delusional happiness,

which imprisons them in fugacity.

They are seduced by sustainable indifference

metamorphosing into themselves.

The Being feels more and more invisible

sinking with each gesture of indifference;

every 'no' that disfigures the skin and destroys hopes.

Humanity hides in the books on the shelf.

The words mark the paper projecting us as

holograms of many shapes and colors —

our brilliance is strong, but ephemeral.

Poems between Bars

The sentence's pain still pulsed when

the cell door closed carrying far away

the dream of hope that deludes the helpless.

The insignificance of those who have always been wrecked

in life, did not enchant the frivolous Judge's eyes;

empathy and segregation inhabit in the same space.

Affliction is immeasurable even to those who build

their stories in foul-smelling places full of

desperate and smiling ragamuffins;

freedom is the only food of those who have nothing.

Jury's men and women (black and white) did not

sensitize with the evidence that should have thrown the

innocent back in the abandoned cold streets

defaced by invisible individuals (undesirable) in the eyes

of those who did not sink under the game rules.

Prison chooses no friends;

concrete walls hurt more than indifference;

violation to an innocent is the worst of all miseries.

The Price of Immortality

Soon the soul will no longer be needed:

micro electronic devices will transform us

into connected individuals without barriers,

without fear of making mistakes.

Fear ... who is afraid these days?

Men and women, women and men, whatever, live in an

irrational and tireless search for something that we cannot build,

let alone buy at the nearest street corner: happiness.

Soon we will no longer have sex:

weird social norms will turn us into

subaltern individuals looking for a deep

social acceptance; vigilantes discriminating their own desires in

favor of a life without taste and smell.

'We will be perfect!' exclaims a UN bureaucrat, who falls

asleep every night before a book on social engineering

he bought in Midtown, Manhattan.

Soon we will be immortal:

individuals — half human half machine —

immune to emotions that expose us to ridicule.

Maybe one day we will no longer need to spend our precious

time looking at an imperfect, old and depressing human face...

a virtual, safe and comfortable life...

how will immortals pay their worldly debts if they are

not forced to face death?

Gears

(Inspired by Chico Buarque's 1971 song "Construção")

He loved her as if it were the last vision

that he would like to stay in his mind.

He kissed her as if it was the last scent

that he would like to stay in his mouth.

And every son and daughter of him as if they were

the only children to inhabit this miserable world

full of stingy adults.

He crossed the street with his timid mind;

a man in punishment with segregated desires

for walls he had been forced to build.

He went up the building in silence — connected with

others to a gear — in a false sepulchral harmony

as if he were about to be replaced.

He raised a solid wall on the landing

to which will one day protect dark interests

those who don't let the gear stop;

brick with brick magically executed

not to frustrate the yearnings of those

who have the right to dream.

With his eyes stiffened in cement

weeping as if he were mourning a stolen life

to feed the insatiable machine that

nourishes our opium of each day.

He sat down to rest as if

he was right to another Saturday:

a perfect day to attenuate problems

in the face of an empty entertainment

mathematically designed to blind
the perception of those who cannot
let the gears stop.
He ate his dog food as if he were
a nobleman accustomed to living
at the expense of his subjects.
He drank and sobbed as if all
his problems were sinking
in waters without vicissitudes.
He danced and laughed as if his ears
were touched by the purest melody,
and tripped on the sky like a man
sloppy full of incurable hurts,
and floated in the air as if he could fly
free as a bird immune to claws
of the parasites that feed on the gears,
and he shattered on the floor
like a mannequin discarded by time.
He agonized in front of passers-by who
confused him for a drunken homeless,
dying in the wrong way, bothering the
traffic of little bourgeois rushed.

Nothing but an Observer

The square is full of young people moving

under another summer sun;

eager as they deprive themselves in their daydreams

without worrying about their own history's lapses.

'Young fools,' thinks a lonely androgynous individual who

rests the old carcass on a discreet bench

under the large tree shadow.

There's not much left but to mock those who have little

life experience craving — more than their own death — the

unhappiness of others.

Young people do not impress themselves about

adults' swindle as they perceive the world in their own way;

youth makes them chaotic, but true.

Life creates monsters when misunderstood.

The elders keep secrets not so

private that can be explained by history —

old precepts marginalized aspirations that sought new

trajectories while a young androgynous exceeded the

limits in a rotten past, even more conservative.

The androgynous isolated themselves

so as not to be destroyed.

Self-inflicted isolation to protect oneself from perversities

dressed as morality that hid the fragility of

a fanatical and unconscious majority.

The constant denial shaped an individual who had become

nefarious so much slaughtering their own feelings.

Psychiatry can explain how retrograde heads

asphyxiate the world of those who feel lost

between male and female afflictions;

of those who sin in the followers' eyes of

a spiteful and vindictive God.

Conservatives are masters of creating freaks....

It is easy to judge the isolated individual who dresses

in a strange way with downcast eyes.

Life loses its meaning when a silent vow

is self-imposed imprisoning oneself in own body;

when the most basic interactions can bare

real feelings refused by a false morality.

The Gardner

Mr. Campbell uses the hoe with difficulty while the master's

grandchildren play on the impeccably cut grass.

He wipes his forehead sweat while his youthful memories

try to surface — there is nothing to remember.

Life sculpted 'servant' before his conception

sealing his fate to the season's rhythm.

He rarely dared to cross the manor's borders

that had welcomed him with open arms.

The master disfigured his personality leaving him mute

and invisible to never live beyond the beautiful garden.

The younger ones don't mind knowing the gardener's name.

Flowers' mutations mitigate the loneliness effects of

a man who knows how to be present without scratching the

beautiful landscape that conceals the nobles' dirty secrets.

Time Machine

From a former homecoming queen to addicted murderer;
a popular, beautiful and outgoing girl sank herself
in the human complexity depths.

White America segregated black people while
warring against the reds to convince the world
that the wonderland was a real place.

The homecoming queen plunged into the acid
to alleviate the anguish of living in a
world fighting for no changes.

The homecoming queen felt the matriarch's conservative hatred
when she was forced to get rid of the child
who grew in her womb.

I would like to go back in time.
A conservative family full of falsified moral values is
a fertile field for the unwarranted hatred.

I would like to go back in time.
A misfit murderers' family has no conscience to
fight the evil behind beautiful metaphors.

Would I stay in the past or kidnap Van Houten to the present
that has benefited from the mistakes of those times?
I would not let the queen destroy herself among scoundrels.

Miles Stripped Bare the White Faces

'So What' filled the jazz house in a way

that would be inconceivable to less privileged minds.

The expressions paralyzed themselves before the black magic

that had invaded the secrets and intimacies resting on those

tables full of big shots, prostitutes and losers —

thinking well, they were all losers....

'Country Son' insinuated that the world was an unrecoverable

place, hypnotizing trained looks for greed.

The music unmasked them while the rot dripping down like

sweat on a white skin face — author of so many atrocities;

they couldn't take their eyes off the stage while the

melody showed them how everything could have been different.

'Miles Runs the Voodoo Down' taught us the right way

for us to free ourselves from the illusion that weakens us

before the individuals who also suffer from bad feelings —

lack of character does not discriminate against skin color.

The waiter noticed the gentleman's hands, which only had eyes

for himself, anxious before the rhythm.

Passers-By

A homeless man pulls over his supermarket cart

so that he doesn't disturb passersby while

he rests the demons that, on a fateful morning, possessed him

on college campus —

the demons manipulated him through LSD.

He had been thrown for decades in a warehouse for madmen

where ambitious researchers tried to reconfigure his

character — they failed. 'This man has no value.'

There is no greater penalty than invisibility;

it is not common for an old white man to get used to not having

a name and face...

he is silent before the shadows that pass by him;

he is ashamed ... it's not his skin color

that threw him out of the system.

He takes chances looking beyond the old cart

full of things that are worth more than him.

It's useless. Only children returned to him:

some of them smile, others repudiate, but he is immune,

because nothing else embarrasses a depersonalized individual.

A police officer approaches him looking at him as if

he was a war prisoner, and says:

'You are obstructing the sidewalk.'

The officer had turned his back on him to greet a gentleman

before the homeless man could answer him, 'Yes, sir.'

The homeless man pushes the supermarket cart into a dirty

alley to rest his body beside a dumpster.

Small Garden

Sunlight shyly illuminates the window

giving him an illusory hope.

His eyes shine disguising a diffused pain,

which exceeds his physical limit, sometimes softens itself.

The desire that feeds that boy's fragile body

sentenced to live in a wheelchair,

imprisoning noble and minimalist feelings,

encourages him to let go of Solitude's hands —

inseparable friend who has been with him since

the suffering childbirth that had killed his poor mother.

If it weren't for the serene and silent Solitude —

who would show him the secrets that insist

in hiding between light and shadow?

Isolation had opened his eyes to stunning

worlds hidden in old pages of such beautiful books.

However, the boy also wanted to share dreams;

he imagines himself feeling all things.

The thoughtful boy becomes able to appreciate

life's movement that moves in a simple garden

inhabited by flowers and radiant insects,

which smile at him every morning, even on rainy days.

His stunted arms struggle to spin the old chair wheels

towards the window that overlooks

the little forest full of insignificant lives.

'Why doesn't the security I give him between these walls calm

his mind?' asks Solitude, when the boy leans in the window to

look at the garden.

'Why don't my reflections calm his heart?' asks Solitude,

when the boy leans on the window to watch

the happy children on the street

as if there was heaven on earth.

Through a small gap of light,

he can see time saying 'goodbye'.

The leaves fall from the trees…

insects dance over the garden…

the lonely boy wants to live beyond the books' pages;

he cultivates desires that Solitude cannot understand:

to extrapolate physical limitations that

reduce him to thoughts and observations.

Solitude is unable to look through the window.

Dear God

A little girl leans over the bed while
the birds chat in a tree near the window.
She does not ignore them. That hoot has a special place
in her mind. 'I feel more alive to my little friends' sound…
another day just for me.'

She drafts a letter full of mixed feelings, which fight among
themselves in the hope that one of them will
emerge victorious to inhabit that future woman.
The hand holds the pen tightly while
words come to life in the small notebook.

Suffering is just steps from the luxury car
that takes her to school every day;
the sight of those poor houses full of
unfortunate people ignited in her an uncontrollable
and childish desire to question the world.

She also records in words the disappointment of seeing
that the world is not so exciting and multicultural
like her favorite TV show.
'Why does the sun shine for me? I don't feel so special.'
The more life the words gain, the more she saddens.

The lifeless boy's body image in the beach hadn't been
enough to interrupt her parents' pathetic discussion about
where they would spend their summer vacation.
The girl doesn't understand that the horrible scene
was the fruit of a strange word: refugee.

The girl understands even less why the reverend
strives so hard to camouflage adults' afflictions
only through a boy god.
'Why does the reverend insist on not respecting the nature?
The world is boy and girl.'

She writes her last words when she sees a
problem: where to send the letter?
God dictates his rules without showing us his face.
'Is there a goddess to whom the girls can send a letter?
Maybe she does help god to help refugees.'

The Boy Who Wanted to Be a Princess

Nathan wanted his parents to build a pedestal

when he still inhabited his mother's body.

The pedestal would help him detoxify his thoughts

so that he could see the world through other colors.

The boy did not understand the embarrassment of building

his aspirations in a world orchestrated to function

in the needy doll's company of welcoming arms.

Nathan was unable to cheer himself when

he was forced to spend his days in a truculent world

full of rude and attractive boys.

The girls were not attractive,

but their world rules were:

there was a commitment to welcome and reconcile feelings,

sometimes confusing for a child.

Dolls made him happy.

The blue world was trying to teach him to be competitive;

however, it forced him to play under oftentimes violent rules.

Nathan decided what to do after falling in love with his

history teacher: 'I will follow my wishes as

my rules. I'm a boy, who loves boys,

but I will play like the girls.'

However, his baseball sticker collection will never be

forgotten — Nathan had learned to love it.

The Girl Who Wanted to Be a Prince

Lynda wanted to get off the pedestal that was built by

her parents when she still inhabited her mother's body.

The pedestal was not all bad,

but it blurred her vision preventing her from seeing

the world through other colors.

The girl did not understand why she couldn't

get down from that orchestrated world to keep her

in the needy doll's company of welcoming arms.

Lynda was unable to cheer herself when

she was forced to spend her days in a compassionate world

full of mysterious and attractive girls.

The boys were not attractive,

but their world rules were:

there was no commitment to welcome and reconcile feelings,

sometimes confusing for a child.

The dolls made her unhappy.

The pink world taught her to be welcoming;

however, it forced her to play under oftentimes obscure rules.

Lynda decided what to do after falling in love with her

science teacher: 'I will follow my wishes as

my rules. I'm a girl, who loves girls,

but I will play like the boys.'

However, her dolls will never be orphaned —

Lynda had learned to love them.

Amnesia

Breakfast had never been so tasty;

the pressure was gone....

All those people around me meant nothing to me.

I didn't hate them, but I also didn't have the

obligation to love them;

'how good it is not to need to love,

how good it is not to have to do anything.'

I just remembered my name and where I lived ——

that was enough!

Enough to enjoy the day like I never had before,

the clock no longer commanded my steps ——

'where would they take me?'

I let my instinct guide me forward,

I didn't need to look back anymore,

I didn't remember my profession;

my job was no longer more important than me.

Me! —— a profound pronoun increasingly ignored by the

modern tasks' selfishness that transforms us into numbers.

Numbers —— damn word! —— a counterpoint to happiness

that had become so demanding that few of us dream

to be able to buy it.

I touched myself. I saw myself in the mirror, but I couldn't say

who I was: my body couldn't define me.

'Did a memory lapse make me asexual?'

This question did not distress me because,

along with the lapse's uncertainties,

came the immeasurable pleasure of an absolute freedom,

which someone consumed by their own

memory demands would never be able to enjoy.

The Depersonalized Girl

Natalie rests her eyes on the school mural on which a small

pamphlet was attached to communicate the party at the

most popular girl's house.

Everyone was invited, including Natalie.

Natalie? Who is Natalie? Ah, Natalie. That strange girl who

keeps her secrets in the school's dark corners.

No! Spectators have no secrets — life for her is just a big

movie filled with depressing characters.

Natalie had been born disconnected from herself;

she has no feelings of her own, because she tortures herself

with the feelings of others — life is a bad drama.

Her reason has not lost facts' consciousness;

however, the pure reason condemns us to be humanoids.

Natalie is invisible: isolated even among the most

unpopular ones — being ignored is proof that someone exists:

loser, ugly, jester….

No, Natalie. She does not exist:

no ambitions, no pain, no desires…

she has just interpreted, better, has observed

what others felt;

she hardly felt her body;

she was unable to feel that shiver in her stomach that other

girls do when they meet the most popular boy.

No, Natalie. The most desired boy is just

a character in a poorly dramatized movie.

It shouldn't be easy to be Natalie; to exist without acting; to feel

things that are not born from her; to witness the victories and

defeats of others … it is desperate not to have her own self.

See You Later

A boy agonizes … he dies of malnutrition.
The Belgian doctor, whose great-grandfather extorted the
wealth from a great property close to the village, couldn't
do anything because the New York-based institution had run
out of funds due to the new pandemic.

A girl breathes hard ... she dies of pneumonia.
The doctor cries beside the rickety body lying on the old
bed in the hope of finding a better destination. The doctor's
conscience weighs on her shoulders when remembering that
the girl's father had died at her grandfather's mining company.

The pandemic advances on the civilized west full of
politically correct people who insist on turning their backs on
illnesses — they're not used to knocking on their doors.
Africa ... thousands of children and adults lose their lives
while another stupid Marvel movie runs around the world.

Africa ... your suffering is proportional to the rhetoric of
those who feel guilty for their ancestors' actions;
Africa ... you are just a special guinea pig for the world owners
to offer camouflaged experiences of benevolence.
The pandemic knocks on our door — see you later, Africa.

Androgynous

The fusion in search of the best of both worlds

to end an endless and stupid war.

A new reality of combining features and feelings

intuited in the late 1960s.

The desire to get rid of old nomenclatures that punish both sides

of the coin:

a social guinea pig sent to wars in which only a private club

that plunders the world is interested;

a social guinea pig indoctrinated to fight against the scales

to die of anorexia nervous.

Everyone loses with that damned division of colors that

symbolize false concepts perpetuated in old scriptures that

prevent us from enjoying inner peace.

The fusion into one being of defects and virtues respecting the

duality necessary to balance energies imprisoned in a world

with sensory limitations.

Was it the end of so much greed and vanity?

The chance to embrace feelings free from labels forcedly created

by a faith that never shows us its face.

Black Gay Lives Matter Too

Brad dodged any form of minutia,

not as common among the boys, when he interacted with his

friends in the old apartment condominium courtyard in an

area of town depreciated by the time and neglected by

those who fear them.

Brad feared letting out the tiniest emotion that was not

compatible with the insatiable need to prove virility and

leadership of a typical alpha male.

Brad felt compelled to imitate them: rough boys addicted to

violent games, trained for urban war.

Brad's father beat him when possible: that big man so weakened

by the emotional wounds of the past blamed his son for all the

bad luck that had embraced his family. It was easier to condemn

him than to hide everyday alcoholism.

'My son will not share the weaknesses of white men.'

Brad's mother went into depression. The drugs doped her,

preventing female embracement, which often arises in the face

of such injustices, destroying any chance of empathy for her

own son —— a miserable community that did not break free from

an amoral taboo.

Brad confided to a friend his desire to break free from prison in which society's rules imprisoned him.

'Hey bro, what are you saying to me?'

Brad suffered his first violence outside his home; the different causes fear for those who hide their own weaknesses.

Brad did not understand how a generation so proud that was leaving the darkness — so full of not neglected voices, which lay bare secular lies hidden in old basements —, still bowed to old patriarchal dogmas.

The basements still hid a lot of dirt.

Brad had been tried by a court of exception, made up of judges unprepared for fear that a small gap could reveal their insecurities. Brad was proud of 'The Squad'.

'Why don't the brothers get inspired by the sisters?' he thought minutes before he died.

High-Tech Vassals

Semi-slaves jobs in some East Asian factory
fulfilled their mission making Tribeca residents
radiant after buying their high-end cell phones.

Tribeca ... beautiful Tribeca ... celebrities' homes;
sensational people so altruistic in their glamorous
speeches before the cameras.

The environment is destroyed somewhere in Latin America,
far from the cameras' glamor, by a northern people mining
company with aggressive sustainability marketing.

Northern people ... an example of equality to minority...
with a deep respect for their forests and natives, they forgot
the sustainability so disseminated in their social networks.

Black Africans: mothers and fathers of the most engaging
rhythms and harmonies that world had known;
civilization's womb — so plundered by benevolent invaders.

Invaders — individuals proud of their social well-being;
civilized people who applaud African artists and athletes who
entertain them in their high-tech tablets.

Artificial intelligence advances on us: robots, cars and TVs
interact with independent self-declared citizens who do not
intuit that they act like high-tech vassals.

Your Ego Is an Asshole

The ego makes you unable to appreciate the beauty that is
hidden around you; it makes you immune to the beauty of
neighbor's garden flowers, which you envy so much...

you are unable to smell the aroma that flowers lend
without wanting anything in return; your ego moves your gaze
only to your own garden — lifeless like you.

The mirror shows you something different than what is in
your mind — you feel special, but you never were;
not as long as you let your ego to dominate you.

Special? Why do you feel that way if you have life in your
favor? Face your ego head on and expel it from
your mind before it destroys you.

The ego feeds on the desire to become a celebrity.
Celebrities are the fruits of the alter ego
of a mentally ill society.

Fear of exposing imperfections, which hide inside your
bowels, feed false perspectives, inducing you to misfortunes
and illusions that will accompany you until your death.

It is a life of implicit denial of yourself;
you look at who is next to you as if you were
destined for stardom...

poor, broken heart...
even those who shine, they are nothing
but cosmic dust destined to disappear.

Adaptation

The day goes away,
night comes to take possession of what is rightfully its,
bringing with it the truth that
lurks behind small formalities.

The bar is full;
drinks and laughs; desperate people
complain about their own lives
whining about what they could have been.

Marital betrayals gain prominence in miserable conversations
narrated under the chords of any song
until someone quotes a sentence disconnected from human
reason of some author cloistered in a filthy room.

Sorrows break free from the minds' entrails of those poor
people dissatisfied with their own jobs.
Mortgage is a word that triggers a feelings avalanche that
lead them to flirt with suicide.

We are not much different from those poor animals slaughtered
in mechanized slaughterhouses.
We are creatures divinely designed to
serve the interests of those who shape our destiny.

We don't want to realize that life has been given to us

only to serve the chosen ones' convenience.

A beautiful financed home or a renowned degree just keeps us

from what we really wanted to be.

How do poor mortals so weakened by their own illusions dare to

stain the mysteries of the night?

Herds should not have the right to free will;

slavery adapts to the time, but it never ends.

The Woman Sitting on the Grave

What was that thoughtful woman doing on that cold and lifeless
stone at Bachelor's Grove Cemetery? She sank into her
memories in search of answers that would never come to her.

The past, yes, her past still bothered her to the point of not
leaving her alone. She couldn't move on and
forget what was left behind.

I married the right man?
Doubts of a badly appreciated past
can be a wound that never heals.

She regretted coming to the world to live under
Christian-patriarchal rules that decided an obscure future
for women — domesticated to live in a marital prison.

She was so stuck in herself that she was afraid to move on.
She let herself be photographed as a form of indignation —
'I want changes!'

The symbolism of the cross and prayers was not enough to
convince her that there was nothing more for her — a limited
existence under dogmas that never did make sense to her.

She was sad. She knew she needed to get up and
move on, but first she would need to make sure
that she would not be deceived again —

if she noticed a small dazzle of falling into the same lies that
she had suffered in life; she would turn her back on the shadows
and she would wander for eternity, but freely.

The Village

A little girl diagnoses a slight cold in the doll.

She comforts her, 'Three rest days and lots of water.'

The little girl knows what she does; she was born to be a doctor.

Boom! A bomb visits the village;

the family dies — her dream too.

The world loses a future doctor thanks to

delusions of those who wish for a better world.

A little boy speaks to himself before a blackboard.

He scribbles things that only he understands;

the little boy knows what he does; he was born to be a teacher.

Boom! A bomb visits the village;

the family dies — his dream too.

The world loses a future teacher thanks to

delusions of those who wish for a better world.

'Who had done such an evil to the poor village?

There was nothing there, except rocks and sand.'

A child, who secretly wants to stop being a child, said,

'Dreaming is a dangerous thing for those who cannot reach it.'

The days pass while dreams persist in surviving

in the miserable little ones' minds,

while childhood immunizes them from the disorders that

misrepresent the elders' dreams.

Where Cowardice Hides

Rosa Parks revealed to the world that the American dream

had never been more than a white dream while

black people lived in an eternal nightmare.

Why did three boys (Chaney, Goodman and Schwerner) frighten

those men so much?

Would it be the fear of facing a new world that was beginning

showing its face?

Fear added mediocrity shaped those

unhappy men who disguised themselves as policemen,

businessmen, judges, workers, Christians, in short,

anything that could help them hide how

insignificant they were...

they were nothing more than coward racists

who feared seeing their women

discovering their first orgasm when seduced by

black men ... racist cowards who feared seeing their sons and

daughters be overcome by black boys and girls —

the strength of Mother Africa who runs through these veins

'would slaughter' those miserable racists unable to project a

non-gray horizon.

History will spit on the graves of those

conspirators and assassins who worship a

fanciful, conservative and vindictive God who loves only

a small group of white men —

history must spit in the memories of those trash humans

whose remains would not even be worthy

to fertilize the simplest and most miserable garden.

Not! No plant or flower would deserve such a nightmare.

Rupture

It is difficult to break free from invisible prisons that
accompany us from conception to death.
Sunday mornings are better,
but they do not prevent that knot in the stomach
that torments me over breakfast.

Children grow as my dreams languish.
They have not yet become aware of the bars that
life imposes on them day after day;
innocence is beautiful, but foolish.
I don't want to meddle — I will let life teach them.

I look at my spouse ... I no longer recognize the
person I married.
I feel like my existence is no longer mine;
as if my goals were mere fits in an
uncertain destiny puzzle.

I want to break free, but I don't know where to start.
'This is a life sentence. When did this happen?'
I move along a no return road not built by me.
My wishes are out of a scene in a movie not directed
by me because, deep down, they were never mine.

Virtual

The young couple in the square with their eyes nailed
on small machines connected from afar with people,
which will never stimulate them the warmth of youth.

The curiosity that so much fueled the charm of youth,
now, it comes to us through connections controlled
by a cold and impersonal artificial intelligence.

The pleasure of feeling alive evaporated like an old and
forgotten ghost as time punished the
face, marking it with small scars.

The next young people will be spared that pleasant
danger, which accompanied us every time
we tried to cheat with innocence.

Innocence ... the seasoning of life that gives flavor to each
discovery; at every step forward before
we destroy ourselves with the nonsense of maturity.

Foolish Adults

The little red-haired boy plays crestfallen in the garden with
an imaginary friend after he had been banned from
visiting the little black girl who lives at the end of the street.

His imaginary friend is loyal, but dehumanized.
It's hard for a child to share worlds and castles
with their own psyche — the little girl is flesh and blood.

The little girl was luckier:
she lessens the segregation's pain alongside Beyoncé,
however, the little boy makes her laugh — the doll doesn't do it.

Children do not understand why the wind and birds
can take their dreams beyond the limits that
the adults impose on them — the end of the street is so close.

'Adults don't know how to make friends. I don't care if
Mike lives in another neighborhood,' says Cathy.
'I don't care if Cathy studies at another school,' says Mike.

One day, Cathy and Mike will learn how adults' worlds
are boring and full of foolish rules to camouflage
old wounds that time cannot heal.

We can only cross our fingers so that Cathy and Mike never lose
the sweet innocence that gives life to the goodness that drives
us to appreciate all colors.

The Owls

The little couple rests on the narrow window sill while looking

inside a huge apartment:

a luxurious home at which four desperate humans to hide their

insignificances fight against themselves to pretend live a life.

The owls camouflage themselves between plants while

the cold, typical of a lonely autumn night, blows tirelessly

on the window glass.

The window sill is always at peace. Down there, the irritating

noises and horns of the cars cannot break the peace of that

Buddhist silence stamped on those birds with big and smart

eyes; they just enjoy the time passing by while

those noisy and strange humans wallow

in thoughts tainted by feelings of self-pity.

The little owls snuggle up against each other to protect

themselves from the cold while they watching the couple of

humans downloading a new 'app' to which will give them the

right to confess online with the priest of their favorite parish.

Those little owls don't understand — never will understand —

the symbolism of sin; and why humans sin so much.

Is it because they are almost always absolved?

The owl family is about to grow. Meanwhile, the birds watch the

couple of children warm and protected in that big

nest; however, behaving as if they were strangers to each other

while their lives are consumed by cell phones.

What sin are they afraid of?

No!

They are too young to be consumed by something

so abstract:

the fear of having to face a debt when confronted

with a god never omnipresent.

Dawn shows its face:

the owls sleep peacefully waiting for another day ... humans ...

they just wait for their miserable emotions to

write the next chapters of a life of appearances full of paranoid

men and women in the face of demands of an increasingly

materialistic and impersonal world, and at the same time,

drowned in dogmas and traditions that prevent them

from seeing how life can (must)

be as simple as a window narrow sill.

The owls sleep soundly...

humans suffer in a nightmare that will

transcend their own death.

Endless Time

Tomorrow seems unreachable:

a little time piece impossible to touch.

The rain falls;

raindrops slide down the window glass.

I call for change,

but I don't know where to go.

Time is slow;

good feelings pass quickly

while anxieties take time to leave.

I remain static:

my mind transcends my brain

beyond the walls that imprison me in simple existence.

I yearn to free myself from what never ends;

everything should come to an end, including the pain.

Attachment pushes us to ourselves;

infinity is the cruelest prison.

The Bird and the Tree

The breeze embraces the faces of those who hurriedly walk so they don't be late for a job, unlike the bird — camouflaged among majestic leaves and branches — that had the privilege of enjoying a beautiful spring day.

'Poor human….' An almost thought was born of a simpleton feeling that emerged in that little consciousness, which takes refuge in the big old tree. The bird does not know envy; however, who would envy those poor creatures?

Collusion

Only words remained;
my days shone before the season's birth;
how good it was to feel the immature adrenaline.

Youthful wanderings encouraged me to
embrace impossible dreams; however, they were true.
How good it was to flirt with life in the company of friends.

The euphoria, which led me to the infinity of each horizon,
degenerated itself like an incurable disease.
I embraced possible dreams; however, they were pretend.

The feelings have aged:
the wanderings gave way to pragmatic routes that
led us into a comfortably unbearable existence.

The yearnings were made explicit by actions;
the words wanted the elders' mouths.
We were free not to bear the wisdom's weight.

The future will remain colluded with the present to isolate me
from my true feelings, which reside in the past ... everyone
blames the time, but that's wrong because we are the traitors.

Slaughterhouse

Innocent lives immune to nightmares hidden in the human
genome, which prevent the simple right to life
of thousands of creatures that are cowardly quartered
in a cold industrial production line.

We are proud to believe that we were
made in the image of a god who never showed us
his own face ... we don't wake up from a nightmare
full of empty and useless sanctities and celebrities.

We are not immune to our own hatred when
we are slaughtered in wars and justified hunger
in a distorted and meaningless reality to serve an
invisible power to the eyes of the poorest.

We do not overcome the eternal slavery that
brilliantly adapts to keep us caged in a gigantic
'big brother' in which tells us what to think, dress and do.
Our real desires are also quartered...

our destiny is not much different from those poor animals.
We also age on a cold industrial production line:
fed to serve the interests of the owners of the world.
Our fear feeds on our pride and alienation.

Our lords do not leave us many options:
heaven or hell, God or Devil, wealth or poverty...
we are more miserable than those poor animals.
We are unable to free ourselves.

Disposable

Creatures that feed on feelings
so fragile in the light of the facts that make them
surprised all the time.

It's easy to compare them to a poorly finished product
contaminated by vile intentions and desires,
which they are masters of hiding.

Nature cannot go back: there is nothing to do but cry with
regret when that insignificant life form, which gave them life,
appears in her memory.

How had an expressionless life form become such a monster? A
routine experience, among many others, spreads like
a cancer over my home.

Where do these feelings come from? I know it doesn't come
from the god they say they worship so much — because he
never existed. I think: 'Which one is the most disposable?'

I (nature) am the great ignored mother. My feelings are not
fragile as those of my ungrateful sons and daughters … all
pandemics were not enough to extinguish them.

What most intrigues me is where do these feelings come
from? My other creations don't live at the vanity flavor.
Where did I go wrong? What should I do to save my home?

Silence

We are losing the ability to dialogue with

ourselves, ignoring loyal friends who express themselves

only when silence silences us so that we can

hear the whispers of help that planet can't get enough

of sending due to the incessant pain that consumes it thanks

to our actions that feed on 'egos' that many

times hide in an addicted collective unconscious

for a human selfishness in a meticulously architected

to expel nefarious thoughts and actions always justified

for an almost divine need for survival that transforms us

into half human-half machine limited to

a little bit of everything and a little bit of nothing.

The Light Goes Out

The photos above the fireplace show me how there was

more light in those days.

At what moment did joy leave us?

We were not suffocated by the daily chores.

At what point did life become our villain?

We plunged into the imaginary up to our lungs' limit.

We were intoxicated by the desire for the impossible,

which named us authors of ourselves.

The youth distanced itself, leaving us with

lying world's memories making us believe in eternity.

Friendships and loves disintegrate faster

than a lifeless body.

It was all just a blowing...

photos only register faces.

Real Feelings (Impossible Loves)

During teenage years' insecurity,
something more was revealed to me than
the simple desire could give me.

It was like a slight awakening...
an irrational need to be
always within reach of her eyes.

What fueled such irrational need?
The simple desire for her body has not disappeared; however,
it has isolated itself in a forgotten corner of my being.

Time was impersonal and impartial when it judged my
dreams disconnected from reality when I fall in love
for someone who would never connect with my strange being.

Teenage years had given way to adult life. Life got more
sober and pragmatic, taking root on my unconscious,
flooding me with old lies propagated as truths.

Life again revealed to me that slight awakening,
not so much now, a little before I bury,
once and for all, my true dreams.

My 'I' was embarrassed of itself every time her
words bared my weakness, which imprisoned me
in the darkest cell of my fragile mind.

That physical-mental confusion went my voices crazy
to the point they never get tired of judging her. 'How does she
dare to invite him to abandon the security of him beliefs?'

Deep down, my voices and I were afraid to dive
deep in that new world that had opened up before my
fragile life.

However, even on the margin, I knew that my world
would never be the same again ... an irrational need
to prove to myself that I would be worthy of her choice.

Yes, 'would be worthy', because at that moment, I knew
that I wasn't; however, my voices insisted on telling me
the opposite...

I'm ashamed to admit ... they convinced me...
the love gave way to hatred, which would be replaced by
indifference — I became even more sober and pragmatic.

Downwind

The problems should be like the wind.

How good it would be to see them

going out the window to dance with the flowers

to just disappear.

There is no unresolved obstacle to the wind;

it can be as quick as thinking.

If we were like the wind, the love pains

would not take root in the memory depths.

No one has experienced such freedom....

Come and go freely without looking back;

be omnipresent while everything else is

bitterly arrested to the feeling itself.

Oh, wind ... take me with you while there is still time.

I want to breathe beyond this room;

I want to fly over the town to see those little ones

desperate points in search of happiness.

Mr. Nobody

Why did you hate yourself so much, Mr. Nobody?
Since you were young, you fantasized about being what
you could never be — never!

You never went beyond the image of a boy
who turned into a man full of hate; ignored, small and cowardly
man ... a pit of lamentations!

Your mother ignored you because she intuitively knew that you
would never be more than a bluffer who always hid
behind the image of a fake patriarch — a hologram!

Oh, lady, how good it was that you hadn't wasted a single
minute of your life with a man who secretly dreamed of being a
beautiful woman ... poor Mr. Nobody...

you would never be able to shine like a woman — to wear
female clothing while you masturbated facing your
victims — you are a grotesque man!

A sadistic man destined to be nobody.
Hatred of women and animals showed the world
a fragile and coward man in the face of his own nature.

You just exhaled hatred to destroy the divine feminine, in
which you, deep inside, dreamed of having (being). You are a
badly finished male design, which will die behind bars.

Internal Voices

I want to hear myself — what does my body have to say to me?

Life has turned into a cold concrete cage.

I'm tired of so many talking faces talking, talking,

but with nothing to say to me.

Only silence is able to let me hear myself

that is arrested in my body.

It is an immense pleasure to sit in front of

the window to watch the rain

bathe the town while I watch the movie that narrates my

life: a bad script with some happy scenes

interpreted by dissimulated characters hungry to

judge my actions — I also judged.

So, I must shut up...

isolation offers me the chance to reconcile myself with

the time, which, when it is right, will get me rid of this

sham script in which I find myself.

The rain is gone, leaving a beautiful horizon behind;

I see the countryside beyond the town:

a plain green shot by insects — so harmonic

as for the flowers that share the same garden:

they do not abhor themselves, because all colors are beautiful.

Finally, my voices free me, more than that, they teach me

that life is like a big dream — beginning, middle and end.

Shhh! Don't throw words into the wind....

Life begs for our attention.

Men of God

Little Oliver did not adapt to the evil that
hid in the cracks of the old school.
The teacher, Mr. Mason, a chaste and empty man
of pleasure, tried to exorcise poor Oliver.

Mr. Mason would never understand that there was no
one to exorcise: Oliver was just a boy
who felt the world through different perceptions.
It is a very high price for a child...

Oliver's parents had no faith in psychology.
Oliver had only one savior: Our Lord Jesus Christ!
'Oliver doesn't behave like a Christian child,' Mr. Mason
told the parents of the misunderstood boy.

Oliver had been left in the care of Father Scott,
who was tasked with teaching him about powers
of the divine grace of a patriarchal God, self-satisfied
with the pain of who he thinks is a sinner.

The weeks turned into months, but divine
grace was not strong enough to free
Oliver from the limbo that tormented him ... but
something different happened…

Father Scott secretly punished himself when

he approached Oliver:

the temptation to caress that pure and

pale skin was stronger than his faith in Christ.

Oliver fell silent. Catatonia had invaded his mind.

With what weapons could a helpless child

defend yourself against a detestable pedophile?

Father Scott gave in to temptation.

Blind faith in an ever-absent God

contaminates even the most natural human

sensations. Christian chastity is a

monster factory.

Oliver couldn't appeal to his parents…

a true Christian would never question

the words of a legitimate representative of God.

Social isolation motivated the boy question himself.

Purity immunizes children's minds, freeing them

of dogmas that only cause unhappiness for generations.

Oliver's innocence was consumed in the same

proportion as his faith in God disappeared.

The House in the Woods

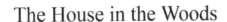

The winding trail took a young addict to an old house that had
been forgotten for decades, full of unhealed memories.
The desperate young man entered the front door looking for
something that maybe he didn't even know he was looking for.

Stunned by the drugs, the young man fixed his eyes on the
portraits exposed over the fireplace not long to hear
the stories that those strange faces wanted to share with him.
His psyche merged with the environment; the voices started....

The little girl's photo, which died from respiratory
complications, whispered to him how the garden was beautiful
during the spring when the family was visited
by a man who played with her in a strange way.

The photo on the side caught his attention: a teenage boy
with an immersed look of panic was looking at him as
if he wanted to alert him about life wasting consequences:
'Our problems do not cease with death,' he whispered.

The couple portrait rested on a wall not far
from there —— they smiled to hide their sins
from the unsuspecting visitors who entered the house.
The old house had buried a suffering world.

The young man left the house smiling with the lightest steps;
his thoughts transcended his own addiction.
Those living memories imprisoned in the portraits
have lit up in him a life hope to be lived.

Leviathan

The sun insisted on being born to those people devastated by
their own dreams — forbidden to dream while humiliated and
destined to be cheap labor for the great democracies.

Children tried to survive while pretending to play on
mountains of garbage imported from those who hold the
answers for all our problems...

'One day I will cross deserts and oceans to free myself from this
country that enslaves me so much,' said a woman, in front of
an empty table with her hungry children watching her.

The president had just been elected: an idealistic person who
suffered while she witnessed chaos reign over the small country
that had been presented with immeasurable natural wealth.

The things seemed to go in favor of the helpless when
the nation was in favor of an old claim: 'Our
riches are ours.' Such words aroused Leviathan.

Hope had been reborn timidly...
the people laughed again when they learned that
they would no longer be enslaved by their own country.

A sunny spring week did not touch
an illustrious messenger who came from a distant and powerful
country avid to sell wealth dreams to the local elite.

The president-elect did not betray herself...

the people were more important than the promises;

the messenger returned, irritating Leviathan.

The people were beaming. After all, old dreams

became reality; children's smiles

no longer wallowed in old promises.

The small country regained its self-esteem a long time ago

lost after the first violation.

Poverty no longer prevented them from dreaming...

the president walks thoughtfully through a beautiful garden

until she falls lifeless to the ground.

The coroner concluded: poisoning.

Chaos was created! Nobody could explain how that

peaceful people suddenly invaded streets and buildings to

destroy their beloved country.

Leviathan shouted to the world: 'We will announce an

agreement to rebuild that poor country. We will guarantee

the security and the logistics of the natural wealth of them.'

Roads and ports filled those naive minds with

pride while their wealth satisfied

the wishes of an insatiable Leviathan.

The time has passed ... the small country was still beautiful,

but more and more miserable and hopeless;

the children wallowed in eternal nightmares....

It was reported to the world that countless wealth had been

discovered in another equally miserable and optimistic country

at which had not learned the lesson with its neighbor.

Leviathan woke up again...

and it was not long before another messenger to disembark,

seducing the local elite with dreams of wealth.

It was an easy job.

The president sold their citizens' dreams for

an amazing trifle.

Leviathan calmed down, but remained insatiable.

The great elite, which always sleeps under Leviathan's shadow,

will always feed on dreams that are not theirs.

Crime and Punishment

Robert Batterson grew up between walls devoid of
attention that every child needs to face all the
monsters that cross our paths. Robert was born
in the rust belt, by the way; he never broke free from there.

Robert hid to wait for time to pass while his mother
leaned over the kitchen table in front of the only
thing that softened her despair: a cheap whiskey bottle;
a dehumanized woman who hated her own family.

Robert spent hours looking through his bedroom window at
hope to find a way out of miserability physical-emotional
that would transform him, still young, in a
menacing man with a fragile spirit.

The nights were worse: the boy's conscience self-destructed,
disfiguring his own psyche, feeding hatred and hopelessness
while he listened to his mother with other men and his father
always absent, losing money in illegal casinos.

A young bully man who ashamed of himself when his own
image was reflected in the mirror — a man of conscience,
disfigured, unable to control the feeling of envy and hatred
against society.

Robert never saw the comfort of a real family
so indispensable to prevent children from becoming
in monsters hungry to propagate human suffering ... a racist,
xenophobic and resentful young man walked among us.

A very rich boy, Shahid, moved from India, awakening
Robert's terrible feelings of self-defense: the fear fed
the xenophobia that fed the hate that fed the envy...
Robert was very fragile...

the teacher introduced Shahid to the class while Robert
consumed himself in a silence full of hatred, capable of
destroying buildings and dreams; start insane shootings;
destroy a life — all this to hide his own failures.

Robert reflected on Shahid during class. He trained a
justification for hating him: a rich foreign kid with
more privileges than me — he was not a Christian!
The perfect argument...

Robert followed Shahid to the school parking lot
where he beat him brutally. He purified himself with each
punch and kick against that pagan foreign boy who dared
to introduce his disgusting god to Robert's beloved country.

Time moved on...
Robert accumulated failures as expected.
It was impossible to make him understand that bullies like
him were already in the process of extinction.

Robert was constantly arrested for drunkenness or aggression

against some peaceful man who had found his place

in the world. He was the father of a boy after

a quick relationship with an unhappy waitress.

Robert eased the pain of his scourge drinking with

failed men in a run-down bar in which even whores

have not put their feet. He left the bar,

staggering, wishing death itself.

Robert's son, Frank, was a sensitive and intelligent boy

loved by the mother; he despised violence and

had eyes for the arts causing shame in

Robert who feared that his son was gay.

Frank suffered bullying at the school of boys who were

the younger version of his father while Robert

ashamed himself before old drinking friends.

He tried to teach his son to be a 'man', but he was unsuccessful.

Frank's mother committed suicide: she cut her wrists. Robert

blamed his son for being gay. The maternal uncle adopted

Frank, leaving him relieved because he no longer needed

to live with a man overtaken by time.

Robert disappeared for years, taking with him

all the misery he accumulated during his life;

a man who failed from the inside out,

alcoholic and unemployed, living with rats.

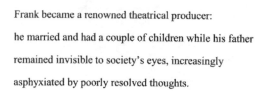

Frank became a renowned theatrical producer:

he married and had a couple of children while his father

remained invisible to society's eyes, increasingly

asphyxiated by poorly resolved thoughts.

Robert stopped at a corner next to an imported

luxury car where Shahid was —

he had become a renowned cardiologist.

Both did not recognize each other ... time moved on.

Shahid was a member of a renowned hospital,

but he also worked for a few hours

a week in a public hospital to help

the neediest.

Robert left another run-down bar in the company of another

loser, Jeff, an old school friend who also

committed bullying. They could barely stand up — reflex

of their own lives.

Frank was beaten, almost to death, by two bullies

because he honked at their old truck that passed the red light,

but the real motivation of so much hatred was

a beautiful Frank's Mercedes.

Frank was taken to the nearest public hospital

in which Shahid saved forgotten lives

by a system that privileges competition.

Frank would never walk without a wheelchair.

Robert entered the hospital half drunk.

He was received by Shahid, who did not recognize him.

Robert forgot about his son when he noticed the little

scar he had done on Shahid's face.

Robert remembered the beating he gave Shahid.

He was also relieved to realize that the doctor

didn't recognize him from school years. Robert felt

proud of that scar —— there was nothing else…

Robert was drinking in the bar when he heard that

the two failed bullies were Jeff's boys.

He hid in the bar restroom to cry

when he finally found out what kind of person he was.

Robert staggered out of the bar towards his house

where he surrendered to cheap cocaine; he whined

more to relieve the pain of his ego than the condition

that Frank was.

Robert sneaked in the back of Jeff's house.

He felt in debt to his son for the first time in his life.

He came in through the kitchen door and killed them both,

bullies who snored on the sofa in the living room.

Robert was sitting on the bed in front of an old mirror

in which he saw himself: a fragile man whose past

had been lost in a mire of shame and irrational decisions.

He felt anger and shame … shot himself in the head.

Synthesis

The words slide smoothly between the lips
of those who captivate them.
Intellectuals rest their bodies in cozy rooms with
the mission of concluding the next thesis about whom
should take the blame for the planet being sick.

Important people mingle in big houses' beautiful gardens full of
sophisticated intellectual hegemony heirs that speak in a
benevolent way — between a glass and another of the most
expensive wines — about the miserable people's afflictions
who survive around the world.

Financiers extend their hands stained with greed to
puppet politicians conceived for obscure deals
in history's eyes, whipping the dignity of
those who don't know how to do anything else,
except humble yourself for survival.

Men and women stay on autopilot
in an endless war to save their miserable jobs.
Intellectuals and politicians around the world lean over
secular issues deceiving immense flocks with the hope that an
antithesis will be born to save them.

Last Breathe

Joseph looked beyond the walls of the hospital room.
His thoughts tried to find a culprit
for the failures of the past ... the lungs started to fail.

Joseph traveled through a discouraging past for someone
who ever believed there was a door in heaven
where all sins would be forgiven.

Joseph landed in the past:
a sad scene in an elementary school in which
he coerces a fat boy to pay him for protection.

The thoughts confronted his reason that
justified itself, arguing that the fat boy
was just a loser — just kidding!

Joseph's reason was wrong because the fat boy,
who wore bottle-bottomed glasses, became a
exemplary father, free from hatred and prejudice.

The lungs started to fail...
the feeling of suffocation increased while
his thoughts traveled through time.

Joseph landed in the past: a presidential suite at
a luxury hotel next to a beautiful prostitute
who counted the seconds to get rid of him.

She pretended pleasure with mastery to the old patriarch,

deluding him to the point that he thought he was a good lover,

while his wife suffered on her deathbed.

The thoughts confronted his reason that

justified itself, arguing that his dying wife

had stopped making love to him — the old patriarchy!

His wife had died alone in the bedroom of a luxurious mansion.

She had loved him in the very distant past, but she always

pretended pleasure like the prostitute did to him.

The lungs started to fail…

the feeling of suffocation increased while

his thoughts traveled through time.

Joseph landed in the past: the old office of

his moving company that he used to

smuggle weapons.

He planned and executed the death of his partner, who

was unaware of Joseph's illegal activities.

'He was stealing from me,' Joseph justified himself.

The thoughts confronted his reason that

justified itself, arguing that a man does what

is necessary to save the business — the old capitalism!

Joseph's reason was wrong because his partner

was always an honest man, often naive,

who opened the door for Joseph when he had no horizons.

The lungs started to fail…

the feeling of suffocation increased while

his thoughts traveled through time.

Joseph landed in the past: a sad memory

from an arms dealer who pushed him into the abyss.

Joseph became poor: he lost his pride and his prostitutes.

He fell into depression shortly before discovering that

he had lung cancer.

The thoughts gave up on confronting him —— guilty!

He returned from the past to the hospital room

provided by the State, which he hated so much.

The lungs could no longer support the body…

Joseph struggled to breathe.

He looked around, but there was no one

to comfort him.

The feelings were confused; thoughts and reason

divorced as his breathing gave way to asphyxia:

Joseph died alone … the world will not miss him.

Small Things

The car crosses the fog-covered road.

The horizon is small, but still beautiful;

everything goes by so fast;

our eyes don't perceive the life's little intervals.

The earth presents us with a rich nature in myths and legends,

which loses strength every anniversary —

we die immersed in our obligations;

our minds become unable to understand the magic.

Time turns its back on us,

because it has been disappointed with us.

Our feet no longer feel the texture of the grass;

imprisoned in shoes that prevent us from

absorbing our great mother's energy.

Great aspirations silence small pleasures that

life gives us for free.

Mrs. Nobody

'Faker! Faker!' said Mrs. Nobody before the

lifeless body of Sylvia, who had been tortured and humiliated

until her life to vanish beyond those fetid walls.

'Faker! Faker!' spit words from a woman's mouth

who had the charisma and intellect of a zombie; a faulty

human project has been expelled by the anus of God.

Sylvia's path has been savagely blocked by a

mediocre woman who would never learn with

her own mistakes…

how did you dare cry in court, Mrs. Nobody?

A coward's tear is the worst of all lamentations.

Evil was your tool to get out of invisibility.

The matriarch of a family whose misery has transcended

the limits of physical poverty. You gave birth,

wickedness in your image, and nothing more.

How does an evil woman be called 'mom'?

Only a society blinded by greed and full of

militancy could tolerate such a fact.

Sylvia's purity and brilliance could have helped a

generation to alleviate the fear of the search for just happiness

so despised by the Jewish-Christian patriarchs.

Sylvia will always be honored, while

Mrs. Nobody will wander in the darkness of oblivion.

The girl just changed shape to enjoy eternity…

Mrs. Nobody will be forever ugly. A fetid spectrum,

unclean, sentenced to be among the real losers:

those who can no longer proceed … move on…

the same goes for those young zombie extras, her children,

which are not worth mentioning their names; all of them

expelled by a big anus — all of them condemned to nothing!

On the other hand, Sylvia suffered, but she transformed herself

to move on — better and stronger! She broke free from

that terrible nightmare, sometimes called life.

The Jurors

The prosecutor imposed before the young defendant accused
of drug trafficking who never crossed the poor neighborhood's
boundaries, in which he was born.

The prosecutor was speaking out loud. Yes, out loud! She was
inspired by her father: a renowned judge who was convinced
that poverty was the result of laziness and lack of intelligence.
'Enough! I do not like irresponsible people. That's why people
like you die miserably,' he told a middle-aged Latin woman,
who was cleaning his summer house, after she was ten minutes
late for work.

The prosecutor felt that the judges leaned in favor of her ideas,
'I'm feeling I'll win again,' she thought as she stared at the
crestfallen young drug dealer with tears in his eyes;
she had felt wrong.

The judge's daughter's arguments, who recently married the
war industry tycoon's son, described universal sentiments
hidden in all those who breathed the same air that occupied that
room ... the jurors were embarrassed by every word spat out
through the imposing woman's mouth —

'Greed! Oh, God. Who at least once in their life did not think of
being as rich as the prosecutor's husband?
The war industry kills more than this poor boy,'
thought a woman (one of the jurors)
remembering the beautiful prosecutor's wedding photo
with her rich husband,
which was stamped on the magazine cover forgotten
on the reception desk of a small employment agency —
the woman remains unemployed.

'Drugs! Oh, God. Hollywood has the monopoly to advertise such addictions in its ridiculous scripts.

How many times have I had to smoke marijuana to be accepted by my friends?' thought a former gang member (one of the jurors), who at sixteen had killed a man during a convenience store robbery —

the gang guy had been acquitted for lack of evidence.

However, hours later, the young drug dealer was convicted; the jurors could not put their fears on the table:

envy, greed and other forbidden feelings should not be embraced by the law's strong arms because they are nothing but dirty secrets. Secrets are secrets....

The prosecutor took a deep breath. She looked at the lawyer as she wanted to make a short speech:

'I won again. My family was graced by God ... I was born with the mission of taking this human garbage off our streets.'

She returned to her manor in a town's noble and isolated suburb while the young drug dealer was taken to his cell.

Justice was done in the eyes of the law ... only the law...

Impetus

Coerced not to act as human anymore

I had only the possession of my thoughts,

which stubborn as always, they ran away

through a small window to meet her.

Before I fall in love with you,

my psyche tames my feelings,

making them nomads thirsty for emotions

intangibles built at the expense of a

self-image mutant as the clouds —

an insecurity that was transmuted

far beyond my body.

Your energy calmed down my impetus (being)

to burn tirelessly in search of the perfect act.

Vibrations

Is there room for me in your thoughts?

Do only thoughts form your character?

Can you see me from the top of your magnificence?

Yes, you can, but you have not sensitized yourself.

Let me absorb your enigmatic world.

To many, you seem cold,

to me, you are indefinable and evasive.

Your talent exceeds the common limits.

Your self-control is enviable.

Once absorbed by your magnetism,

I have coveted (I need it) to be worthy of your thoughts;

perhaps one day, I will be worthy of your body.

My psyche (charlatan), in the past, immune to human ills,

spuriously stately before the real life's stumbles,

has melted towards your sagaciously sensual intellectuality —

the beauty beyond-body.

My pride and innocence burnt my wings.

The rapture consumed me, destroying my fragile 'I';

I have tried to follow your light. Poor me!

Your brown eyes have undressed my thoughts.

My theater collapsed, melting my masks as if I were a sham.

What to do? Your conscience has seized my being:

if you think, therefore I am.

You destroyed me (rebuilt me) — I am part of you.

Gallery

The art critic got out of bed elegantly when he felt
the first rays of the sun caress his face artificially,
stretched to cover the time.

His breakfast had been quiet until a newspaper note
transported him to the real world that so insisted on stripping his
indifference about the inspirations of those he criticized.

The art critic did not contain his emotion before the moribund
woman's photo — whose story was erased — resting her
old body, almost lifeless, while she hindered the traffic.

'Poor woman,' he said as he finished his breakfast.
However, he quickly forgot about her when he remembered
the gala event that he would have that night.

Part II

The Gala Event

Celebrities lined up before a beautiful work of art:
another beautiful painting by a renowned artist, depicting
human anguish … suffering is inspiring.

The art critic's mind collapsed into orgasms

before so much beauty and creativity. 'What inspires so much

beauty?' he envied, in a transparent act of inferiority.

The art critic rationalizes shapes and colors;

nothing escapes his methodical gaze. And

his words inspire the ego of collectors.

The artist swerved out his way by exchanging human pain

for the individual pleasure of glory: someone like that

poor woman had been forgotten.

Post-mortem

It wasn't so bad...

my conscience had erased before my lungs stopped;

in a short time lapse,

I wake up to strangers with friendly features...

I breathe like I've never done before.

I no longer feel the old obligations' burden.

I am no longer a slave to a mundane life full of obstacles.

I find some familiar faces again;

strange ... the grudge was gone...

they explain to me that not everyone

will go through such an experience:

'Existence is like the land:

learn to plant and look where you step.'

They show me my temporary home;

peace reigns between those little walls.

The neighborhood is, like everything else, a plural society;

all colors and expressions are welcome.

My dogmas almost don't bother me anymore:

they will become harmless dreams,

which my psyche will soon erase.

I still feel desires accompanied by worldly thoughts;

a friend explained to me,

'It's normal. Your body will give way to your mind.'

I grew to understand them:

it takes time to heal the mind;

I was lucky — my ego was small.

Disappeared

Personal furniture and objects do not get tired of waiting

for the return of the person who gave meaning to their psyche.

Parents watch on the news in the hope of reporting

any clue, even if that is a body thrown

in a dirty and miserable ditch.

Time does not miss those who are gone,

not caring about the story behind them;

for time, everything is just another photo,

forgotten in an old chest called life.

Follow Morning

The change fear haunts me every time

I rest my intolerant eyes to witness

the transformations that advance over my face.

Fear: damn perfect fuel to fill the human

cockroach's mind unable to break free from

own moorings passed down from generation to generation,

by reason of old prejudices.

Prejudice: putrefied thought that sickens the intellect

who, conscious or not, suffers his own existence's pains.

I feel arrested and unable to harmonize with myself before the

differences, which give life to those who oppose me.

Skin color; self-declared gender; foreign accent; or

someone who just doesn't submit to the holy book rules —

why do I need to hate them?

My mind cries out for that.

I am unable to understand how despicable I am.

I fall from grace in my dark days

while others learn to bury old ghosts.

The world is more beautiful when the mortals overcome

history's mistakes —— free yourselves to experiment;

poor conservatives...

the horizon is reborn for those who are not afraid to change.

Death Is a Second Chance

PROLOGUE

Mr. Ross felt the wind caress his old face as he looked at
the beautiful landscape that welcomed his balcony;
nature's silence was perfect for him to drown the damage
psychological that loneliness produced in his mind.

Time passed while he brooded over old wounds
that insisted on inhabiting his imagination.
Repentance accompanied him from an early age, not
letting him forget that he made all the decisions.

He was just minutes away from facing death itself.
Intuitively, he knew it was; however, he kept serene before
the inevitable — serenity obstructed the actions of the
his emotion making him submissive to his own reason.

His reason was a selfish ally that programmed him for
living like a machine — machines suffer loneliness.
His psyche did not view reality as the psyche of
Nietzsche; however, both them sailed on similar dogmas.

Only death could free him from the old memories that
put him in front of the wall, staining a life trajectory
that only cared to satisfy the demands of his own
reason, strengthening the mind at the expense of the spirit.

He looked within himself, but he never accepted the
own feelings as an integral part of his own being, which
didn't make him any less worthy; however, too mechanical
to act in the face of the subtleties of life.

Death patiently waited him to finish the journey
he had done so many times throughout his life without
reaching a conclusion about which decision he should have
taken: three women could have freed him from this agony.

The time has come: death had put its hand on his shoulder
to take him on a trip that could transform him forever,
whereas that, he learns to understand the minutiae
of his own psyche.

I

A child leaning over mystery books, trying to escape
the bitter taste that reality never gave up imposing
about his fate. His thoughts could travel
without worrying about the boys' rules of survival.

Charles Ross knew very well how to get rid of the traps
of an infantile male universe, composed of rude and selfish
boys who will metamorphose into violent and drunkard
men, which are slowly moving towards extinction.

Charles perceived the world through clumsy intuition.

He knew that things were changing for the better

when Aida, an exotic girl, joined his friends

to impress them with her old skateboard.

Charles was impressed as Aida born prepared for

facing, within the rules, the boys' distrust, which

imprisoned them to a future that will soon be gone.

Aida ignored stereotypes by writing her own script.

Aida was a girl, and as such, she was despised by

the girls, which they did not give up protecting with

tooth and nail the false image of their alpha boyfriends:

an alpha boy is a valuable trophy for a popular girl.

Charles admired Aida while the majority envied her. 'Aida is

smart, sweet and strong. She does well in everything she does,

but without belittling those who respect her,' thought Charles,

when she sat next to him in chemistry class.

Aida liked Charles. She liked silent and introspective boys

instead of those assholes who chase after a ball and

laugh about anything. Charles had a little

bit of humor that made him even better.

Charles was not open to his emotions, censoring them

whenever he could — life offered him a light beyond

the logical temporal limits of his reason.

Charles was afraid of falling in love...

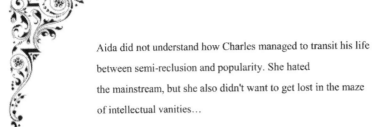

Aida did not understand how Charles managed to transit his life between semi-reclusion and popularity. She hated the mainstream, but she also didn't want to get lost in the maze of intellectual vanities…

Charles's emotion knocked on his consciousness door several times to alert him of an evident separation: the passion of the couple has cooled and each of them took refuge in the most secret little room from their minds.

Charles's reason was silenced ashamed because it did not manage to formulate a logical solution, while his emotion speaking at full speed, trying to convince him not to act anymore in this way ... Charles cried all night…

his future could have been incredible with a girl who longed for a co-author to write her script (both) without fear of venturing freely across all physical and mental hemispheres.

II

Charles had been consumed by the passion for knowledge; it could not have been different because he continued his trajectory within the limits of his own reason, becoming a young man recluse with a friendly aura for some women.

Charles succumbed to the passion for an intriguing young woman, Maya, for whom, perhaps for the first time in his life, he gave due attention to his emotion, which it was shy, almost giving up on him, but Charles was still Charles.

He studied economic science; however, together with
maturity, his passions became philosophy and
psychiatry. He was freer from his own dogmas,
but he was still pragmatic.

Maya had as a principle to harmonize with the two
sides of the same sphere that made her love psychiatry;
she was a renowned and happy psychiatrist, while Charles
had become a successful financier, but an incomplete person.

Maya transcended the simple with a desire to venturing into
life and herself. She was able to reconcile the little ones myself
who cohabited in her psyche —
understand yourself to understand the whole.

Charles and Maya completed each other under the sheet sets,
but that wasn't enough: love disappeared. Charles's future could
have amazing next to a woman who could have set him free
from his mental boundaries from which he was afraid to cross.

Charles was rich, but he was sorry to feel empty.
He still felt unable to reconcile the little ones myself
who lived in conflict in his mind, leaving him lost among
happiness and unhappiness — a difficult place to leave.

Charles was an assiduous middle-aged man frequenter

of public libraries to quench the thirst for knowledge,

from which he inherited from his youth.

Charles had become dehumanized…

libraries were almost always lifeless, but Charles

in the innermost of his most secret desires, he believed one day

to find the last chance for him to try be happy: find

the female version of himself — same virtues and defects.

Jade was reading Hegel when Charles sat next to her with

a collection of poems by Sylvia Plath. It was instantaneous:

they loved each other at the first blink ... the third chance was

born in the woman's shape whose conscience was compatible.

Jade had achieved one of the dreams that Charles left in the past:

philosophy. She was a professor at a renowned college...

they loved each other even when silence interrupted them to

inform them that it was time to dialogue with their emotions.

Charles and Jade spiritually merged into one person: a cerebral

middle-aged couple who learned to give voice to their own

feelings. She never turned her back on her emotion;

however, she let her own ego blind her.

Charles did not take long to discover that emotion once again

had been left out because both could not destroy

the best version of themselves to give way to a new 'me',

so essential to giving birth to a new 'we'.

Jade had a more possessive conscience because
she knew how to play with her own feelings when
destiny of her decisions was for herself.
Part of Charles's consciousness had been altered.

Charles was transformed. Part of his world perception
changed according to her philosophy; however, this was not
enough: the spiritual fusion broke up.
Their pride prevented them from being happy.

Jade is gone. Charles gave up on public libraries,
because he intuited that the answer to his problems
was not to find his female version, too
less would be in the books...

Charles felt incomplete: once again, he failed
when was necessary to harmonize the two main
elements that formed his mind: the old conflict
between reason and emotion...

Charles could have loved and been loved by a woman
who understood him like no one to the point of
transforming him so that both could understand
the beyond-mind: spirit and destiny.

Charles gave up fighting himself.
He finally understood that he was a dictator
of himself, not giving voice to his own feelings.
He suffered between happiness and unhappiness...

EPILOGUE

Mr. Ross died alone on the balcony of his mansion, but he had been knocked unconscious before he could have seen the face of death; by the way, death never shows its face. Charles died, but he had not paid off his debt to himself.

A thought. An unease followed him through the beyond-body transition: which option, or rather, which of the women could have been the right way to help me with the dictatorship that my own reason caused to me?

Charles returned to his own conscience alongside people who he had met in life: his paternal grandfather and a childhood friend. He quickly noticed that he was in the same balcony — he had become too attached to that house.

They told him that his parents could not be present because both had reincarnated. Charles walked alone to the living room, where to his amazement, Jade was sitting on the couch. He sat next to her...

it was impossible to contain the tears ... silence reigned for a few seconds, answering the question that has accompanied him beyond-body: Jade was the right option. Both needed to reincarnate so they could finish their mission.

Charles felt a peace he had never felt when he was a slave of his own reason: his emotion broke free ... they kissed and spent the rest of the afternoon hugging each other in front of fireplace.

The Stage

Small memories, commonly despised,

do not dissolve in the mind of a forgotten being.

A smile, even if ephemeral, can take root

deep and painful to someone who acted little.

Friendly conversations of yore disappear

in the time dimension,

but not for someone who hasn't been able to

free themselves from a non-glorious past.

The individual ages:

death throws itself on the psyche, then the body.

Time is summed up in a dusty photo album

it's all that's left to the disdained one.

There is no other refuge for someone who

did not know how to act;

life is full of characters that hide

behind dazzling, but narcissistic masks.

Being-Nothing-Becoming

Dawn brings life to flowers, even those

that fall apart before the existence through death.

The sun warms the soil, instigating the present to draw

a future as uncertain as the boundaries of the absolute.

The sensation of emptiness merges with a shy perception,

unable to reveal to us the tenuous line

that precedes existence.

The apparent chaos that is camouflaged in the dimension of

infinity, which architect the absolute before

it can seize our minds, confusing us to

intuit that 'becoming' has its own psyche:

a small energetic-elementary worker acting

simultaneously between 'being' and 'nothing' slowly,

or better, eternally, revealing us forms and

concepts that gravitate around our imaginary.

Darkness brings rest to flowers, even those that

headed towards 'becoming' thanks to the small workers

capable of acting even in the coldest of the vacuum...

Kids Facing the Wall

Childish daydreams amputated by iniquitous judges

comforted in beautiful homes with white fences;

some not so beautiful.

Agonizing little individuals daring to crave

a world little piece beyond-wall.

Children, others not so much, born under a servile ethnicity

unworthy to share the happiness of

those who consider themselves new

world's owners, perhaps, the whole world.

How to explain the cultivation of such an execration?

The chosen ones who savor paradise sleep in fear

and wake up possessed by hate — degrading!

The wall had been born from a nefarious

collective consciousness averse to the plural's beauty;

the hatred of the different vernaculars, colors, and faces.

Children cross deserts and oceans searching for the perfect place

so disseminated on the screens by false heroes and heroines,

which further contaminate the minds of those who

strive to survive in an exotic and fetid world's storms —

the screens make us believe that

there are no walls beyond-wall:

a paradise full of white fences and beautiful gardens.

The old speeches' leaders change like the seasons;

children grow old, but the wall will persist!

Afrotranscendental

The circle of life is endless as mistakes and hits

confront each other in the mind of a poor mortal.

The desire for the tangible overflows common sense, leading

humanity to suffer slowly.

Artificial intelligence advances on us, replacing the value

of consciousness, making us forget the spirit.

The brains of the machines will erase the essence that

guides us through winding roads because machines are

devoid of spirit and they don't pay for

their mistakes, much less repent for them.

Our mission is to break free from the circle

so that we can move on.

Only the spirit can break the barriers of this endless circle:

Mother Africa has shown us the way through African religions.

Yes, it is possible to talk to the dead.

Higher consciences are at our disposal with their hands extended

so that we can intuit the truth.

Racist people insist on pretending to love a false god, almost

always patriarchal, so that they can hide an immeasurable

feeling of inferiority through hate, greed, and denial of our

greatest strength: the spirit.

Mother Africa has given us the greatest legacy of humanity, but

most have no conscience to admit it.

Configuring People

The teacher is satisfied at the end of the day to see her
little students leave the room aware of
another good social conduct rule.

She had taught them that the world would look like a great
playground if we all cooperated so that no one was evicted
from their own purposes.

The teacher is convinced that her words transcend
the school's walls like small waves that
turn into a powerful 'tsunami'.

The warrior knows that it is necessary to domesticate the small
ego, which inhabits each child, in order to combat the
vicissitudes that so punish our fragile harmony.

The alphabet sung at the top of their lungs —
correct attitudes hand in hand with ideals that plead with
children so that they can enter their hearts.

The little ones have returned to their homes...
the teacher fixes her hair in front of the dressing table
not failing to notice the signs of aging.

She is not saddened to see time has gone by
in a small room while the little ones
grow into life without looking back.

Miracles configure themselves in flesh and bone in those rooms
in which battles are won, one at a time, so that the history is not
written by those who think they own it.

The Incarcerated

Surrounded by hatred and regret, I felt on my skin
the horrors that hide in the human labyrinth
existing in each one of us.

I fell silent in the face of social pain in exchange for an
execrable survival built under the rhetoric that has
bombed me since the orgasm that imposed life on me.

The inconsistency between facts and words made me see the
invisible bars that imprisoned my psyche limiting
my real yearnings in the vassal melody's rhythm.

I felt ashamed when I was imprisoned with myself.
The all prisons mother has caused me a painful abstinence
able to break myself free from the mainstream claws.

I regained my free will against a hegemonic
thought that treated me like a part of gear.
My thoughts will not be lost in emotional labyrinths.

Somewhere in Time

I don't remember where I hid that little bit of memory,
so tiny, but attractive to the eyes of others that
watched avid to judge me.

Where are those eyes now?
Probably feeding on the weaknesses of others,
but unable to put their own pieces together.

My second 'me' — obscure even to good perceptions —
shames me to the point I surrender my whole story to the
dark side, which never asked me anything in return.

I reconstruct my memories — piece by piece.
The more dust, the more embarrassing will be the
feelings that built my path.

Time is indifferent to my stumbles;
it is up to me to face them without self-pity,
no constraints, which bare my face.

I feel better: I breathe easier with each open
file drawer granting me to know myself better;
I am imperfect, but not abnormal.

I invigorate myself with every bit of memory found.
I free myself to assume mistakes and betrayals, no shyness;
I understand that those who judged me failed as well.

Rooms and Secrets

The sun opens another morning.
The houses are silent before the horrible
revelations they witness
every generation:

the living room's couch still contains
sperm residues from the last marital betrayal.
The young wife had gone crazy when she felt
the orgasm energy for the first time.

The young couple almost lost their lives
in their last overdose on Valentine's Day.
The girl had learned to enjoy cocaine with her mother:
a respected doctor who had become addicted during college.

The nurse physically abuses an old man
unable to express who has been left to die
in a filthy room by his single son who abuses
the nurse sexually.

A Catholic woman, who loves Jesus above all,
lost the newborn baby in a clandestine abortion.
Her parents do not imagine that the child's father is a
bisexual priest acquitted in a child abuse case.

The sun opens another morning.
The houses are silent before the beautiful
revelations they witness
every generation:

an elderly couple rejoiced when they heard
that their grandson, who had been arrested
for drug trafficking, had won a scholarship for
a renowned educational institution.

Flying over the Secrets

The old house was still imposing on the rocks
punished by the waves' crash.
Old walls witnessed secrets in the form of voices,
moans and cries, dissimulated by smiles and hugs
tightly and minutely architected to hide desires and
parallel perceptions born in repulse.

A false harmony overlapped itself over those thinking
heads: portraits on the fireplace displayed only
the surface of those who smiled at the history —
fruitless lives fertilized with narcissism,
which dodged from the cameras' lenses;
an almost perfect hoax.

The meetings at dinner time were the most
obscure moments, perhaps the most dangerous.
Poor children ... childhood made them immune to the elders'
ills and vicissitudes, but they will become adults
with visions scrimped to their own needs —
the history told by those who have no history.

The most sensitive heads are quick to notice the dialogue lack
amidst so much banal conversation between adults
desperate to hide their insignificance.
Primitive desires, when not contained, sew pathetic beings;
possessive adults full of self-pity.
The being shies before the having.

Made in the USA
Columbia, SC
08 January 2023

75798404R00071